D0352657

This
Harry and
the
Dinosaurs
book belongs to

. . . .

SCELIDOSAURUS

(ske-LI-doh-SAW-rus)

TYRANNOSAURUS

(tie-RAN-oh-SAW-rus)

TRICERATOPS

(try-SER-a-tops)

STEGOSAURUS

(STEG-oh-SAW-rus)

PTERODACTYL

(TER-oh-DAC-til)

APATOSAURUS

(a-PAT-oh-SAW-rus)

ANCHISAURUS

(AN-ki-SAW-rus)

It was a long drive to the safari park but it was worth it.
Apatosaurus saw an animal just like Triceratops.
"That's a rhinoceros," said Harry.
"Triceratops has got more horns."

Mum liked the giraffes best and Nan
liked the zebras.
    The monkeys were funny but the
man said not to feed them.

Sam asked him if they had pandas but the man said no, they were endangered animals.
Harry wanted to know what endangered meant.
Sam said he was too little to understand.

Nan helped. She bought Harry a book about endangered animals. She thought it was sad about the Sumatran tigers. People kept hunting them so there were only a few left in the whole world.

Harry really wanted to help but he had no money.
  "I want to save some animals," he said.
"What can I do, Mum?"

Sam said, "Tuh! What a waste of time!"
She said he was miles too small to make any
difference. That's why Harry made her do a smudge
with her lipstick.

Mum took Harry off to settle down.
Then they looked on the Internet
and found lots of endangered animals.

Mum said why not do a poster? Harry could put it up in his window. Then maybe other people would help the animals too.

Harry liked that idea. He got out his drawing stuff straight away. Trouble was, it was hard to know which animal to save first.

The dinosaurs said, "Raaaah!
We want to save some BIG animals!"

So they started drawing.

Tyrannosaurus did a polar bear.

Pterodactyl asked Harry to help him do a gorilla.

"Wait till I've finished my blue whale," said Harry.
"Blue whales are bigger than trains, bigger than
dinosaurs, bigger than thirty-two elephants!"

Stegosaurus did an army tank.
"Army tanks don't need saving!" said Triceratops.
"Do a tree frog instead."

Mum said the drawings were excellent.
She helped put the words on.
LET'S SAVE THESE ENDANGERED ANIMALS!

Nan said, "Why not talk to Mr Bopsom?
He might put up a poster in his shop window!
Then people can see the pictures when they go shopping!"

Mr Bopsom loved the pictures but he thought they might
be a bit too small for a poster.

He asked Harry if he could draw them bigger.

Harry said no, sorry, his pictures always came out small.

"That's a shame," said Mr Bopsom. "Because saving animals is important!"

Poor Harry. He went home feeling maybe Sam was right. Maybe you had to be big before you could be any use.

The very next day, Mr Bopsom was on the phone.
"I've had an idea!" he said. "Can you do me *lots* more pictures?"

So Harry and the dinosaurs did more birds
and bugs and reptiles
and *lots more dinosaurs!*

Then off they went to give them to Mr Bopsom.

When Harry went into the shop two weeks later
he was amazed! Mr Bopsom had made all the
drawings into cards.

   He said that every time somebody bought a card,
some of the money went to save endangered animals.

Everybody loved them. They said, "Marvellous!"
    "What a brilliant idea!"
    "So original!"
    "Four cards for me, please!"

The lady from the paper came and was very impressed.

"What a wonderful thing you've done!" she said.

"Raahh!" said Apatosaurus. "Save the strawberry poison arrow frog!"

"Raahh!" said Pterodactyl. "Save the teeny blue tongued skink!"

And Harry said, "Quite right, my dinosaurs! Because even if you are as tiny as a tick on the tail of a green turtle, you can still do something that makes a BIG difference!"

ENDOSAURUS

SCELIDOSAURUS

(ske-LI-doh-SAW-rus)

TYRANNOSAURUS

(tie-RAN-oh-SAW-rus)

TRICERATOPS

(try-SER-a-tops)

STEGOSAURUS

(STEG-oh-SAW-rus)

PTERODACTYL

(TER-oh-DAC-til)

APATOSAURUS

(a-PAT-oh-SAW-rus)

ANCHISAURUS

(AN-ki-SAW-rus)